It's Only Annie!

It's Only Annie!

Tony and Jan Payne

Illustrated by Rosie Reeve

Dolphin Paperbacks

First published in Great Britain in 2005
as a Dolphin Paperback
by Orion Children's Books
a division of the Orion Publishing Group Ltd
Orion House
5 Upper St Martin's Lane
London WC2H 9EA

1 3 5 7 9 10 8 6 4 2

A catalogue record for this book is
available from the British Library

Printed in Great Britain by Clays Ltd, St Ives plc

ISBN   1 84255 159 0

www.orionbooks.co.uk

This is for Margaret Meek,
who we have known and loved for ever

Contents

Annie First

Why is cleaning up my room such a big thing?

I like all my stuff where I can see it, on the floor and on my bed. It's not as if anyone wants to go into my room except me. Dad makes the bed most of the time and sometimes brings in the Hoover, but I don't think he really knows much about hoovering. He can switch it on, but then spends more time trying to figure out what the knobs are for than actually doing anything.

"What does this little drawing mean, then?" he asked once, as if I'd know!

"It looks as if I'm supposed to throw the Hoover out of the window!"

"Go on then," I said. That would be more interesting than watching him wave it around the middle of the carpet like he normally does. There's more dust around *after* he's cleaned up.

"That can't be right," he said. "I think I'll just throw the carpet over the washing line and beat it up with a stick. That's what your grandmother had to do when she was a girl."

He meant Gran Weatherburn. I have another granny, Granny Fidgen, who is very posh and has never ever had to clean a carpet. Gran was a girl a really, really long time ago. But even though she's old now and has veins on the outside of her legs, she knows how to use a Hoover, *and* how to take one to bits and put it back together again. Dad's not good with housework though, or machines, but he's good with computers, I think.

"Your grandmother used to be in the Brownies," he said. "She got Brownie points and 5p for doing things like washing up and cleaning her room – and beating carpets."

5p for cleaning a whole room?

Then Dad looked at me and his eyes lit up, and I *knew* what he was thinking.

"No, Dad!" I pleaded.

"Yes, Annie!" he said. "It's the Brownies for you."

It's just not fair! I *never* join anything. I don't want to be with a lot of other kids. I like just being me. On the day Dad thought of his *brilliant* idea to get rid of me by packing me off to the Brownies, Mum was off on one of her adventures, otherwise I might have got out of it. Mum's got a guilty conscience because she's not around more, so when she is home I usually get my own way. She was home the day the Brownies met though, so she took me in her car. It's an old French car, made of plastic. It doesn't have any sides or back, and it has a cloth roof. It sounds like it's doing two hundred miles an hour, but someone could overtake it pushing a piano, so Mum says. She loves it to bits.

The Brownies' place was really just a big
wooden hut, and over the doors and
windows were flags of different countries,
put out to dry on a washing line. Mum gave
me a hug, dropped me off outside, and
drove off . . . to Russia this time.

A smiley lady wearing a big school
uniform and socks rushed over when I
walked in. She said she was called *Brown
Owl*, which was a silly name, I thought.

I had to stand in front of everybody and say who I was and where I came from. I was the only one there not wearing a uniform. Mrs Owl gave me some paper and magaziny things and sent me to sit at a bright red and blue table to look at them.

There was a blank sheet of paper, and I was supposed to write down things about myself – what my favourite colour was and stuff like that. What were my interests? I couldn't think of any. I've got too many things to do to have *interests*.

Then I looked at the magazine. It had the uniforms and stuff, and they weren't bad. There was a nice gilet top, a hoody and a baseball cap, but no way was I going to wear something called a 'skort'. Also, I didn't like the colour; it was bright yellow! I'd look like a road mender in a bright yellow gilet.

Over the page it showed some of the things that Brownies and Guides did. This was more like it! There was go-karting, snorkelling, pony trekking, canoeing — all sorts of cool things. I'd be doing some of the things Mum does — quad biking, rock climbing . . . *hang-gliding*!

Well, I didn't think I could do all those things straight away, maybe next month, but I couldn't wait to find out what we'd be doing that evening. I asked Mrs Owl, and she said we were all going to learn the proper way to wash our *feet*.

I thought she must be joking! "What about scuba diving and stuff?" I asked.

"It's very important to take care of your

feet," said Mrs Owl, still smiling. She was never *not* smiling. "We do all those activities in the brochure on special outings, but you can't do any of them if your feet aren't healthy. Don't forget we have the parade on Saturday. You're going to need your feet."

"I didn't know there was going to be a parade," I said.

"Ah, well, this is a very special year for us, Annie. It's our *ninetieth* birthday, and this weekend the Guides and Brownies are having a grand parade together. Cubs and Scouts will be having theirs as well, as we all share the same birthday.

"There'll be colourful floats and marching bands, and all sorts of wonderful things. Even the Band of the Royal Marines will be coming! The television cameras will be there – and this is the best bit, Annie . . . our little troop will be right at the front of the procession. Won't that be fun?"

Well, yes, more fun than feet-washing lessons, definitely. We still had to do that though, and draw on the floor around our

feet with a felt-tip pen, and then look at pictures of the shoes our feet liked best.

Mrs Owl asked me what my main interest was, so that I could have a badge. I chose cloth dyeing – you know, dyeing cloth different colours. OK, I know I couldn't think of anything before, but I had to pick something, even if my main interest wasn't that interesting.

By the time we packed up, I'd learned how to wash my feet; tie a knot; written all about *me* – and joined in a 'powwow'. I was dying to be let out when Gran came to pick me up.

I went with her to Wearsons department store the next day to get my Brownie uniform. When I got home I looked up the instructions for my new "interest" – cloth dyeing. Then I shoved the uniform into the washing machine and added the coloured dye I'd bought. I wanted a blue uniform, but when the clothes had finished whizzing round at last, I'd got a green one instead. That was all right. I wouldn't look like everyone else. That was the most important thing.

On Saturday I went to the parade meeting. Mrs Owl looked amazed at my nice green uniform. "But Annie, it's not our pack's colour!" she wailed.

"You said I could choose the clothes I wore if they were in the book," I said.

"Yes, but not if they were a different colour! Oh dear, what are we to do with you? The procession starts in a few minutes and there's no time to find other clothes."

She looked at me, thinking hard. "We're going straight up the high street to Hingham Park. It couldn't be simpler. Do you think you could lead the parade?" she asked.

"Yes," I said. "That's easy."

"Good girl. People will think you're dressed differently because you're at the front – the leader of the pack! I'll be at the back with another group, I'm afraid, so I won't be able to keep an eye on you, but I know you'll be fine."

A big pack of Guides arrived then, and some other Brownie packs, and the floats were lined up ready to go. There were a lot of them. One looked like a big purple dragon on wheels, tossing its head and breathing out flames and smoke. It was playing a little jingly tune. We all knew it was Mr Alexander's ice-cream van in disguise, because he can't turn off his jingle and people round here know it well.

Drinks were handed round before we started, and everyone was given a huge tub of sweets. It was getting exciting, actually.

The soldiers' band was right behind us. Its huge bass drum got us going.

Boom . . . boom . . . BOOM, BOOM, BOOM, BOOM.

Then the rest of the drummers began tapping away and the other instruments started playing. The noise was amazing.

And I was right at the front. *Annie first – yeahhh*!

I had to walk fast, because the band kept bashing into us if I didn't. But we didn't have to march in step like them. I walked in the centre of the road, waving to the crowds and turning round and round, so I could see what the others were doing and do what they did. I really got into it. The tub of

sweets was
for throwing into the
crowd, and I was very fair
dishing them out – one for
them, one for me, one for them,
one for me ...

But then I had a problem. The
high street is quite long, and I'd had a
lot to drink. I was *dying* for a pee. I tried
to hold on, but it was getting serious. I
yelled to the Brownie behind to keep going
and that I'd catch up later, then I dashed
into the main hall of the big supermarket
we were going past. There was a queue at
the toilet, and I was desperate by the
time I could go,
but I could still
hear the band,
quite loudly, so I
knew they hadn't
got too far ahead.

I was in for an
enormous shock when
I came out!

21

The parade had followed me into the supermarket! All the Brownies and Guides were milling about not knowing what to do, and most of the band were marching on the spot. No wonder I could still hear the band from inside the toilet – they were just on the other side of the wall! The sound was *deafening*. It rattled the windows, and trolleys jiggled about all over the place.

The floats had tried to get inside too.

They must have just followed the one in front and not looked where they were going. The large dragon was stuck at the entrance, his head snapping and breathing fire, and still playing *Nellie the Elephant*. The man with the big drum was outside, but his

drum was *inside*, jammed in a revolving door. Nobody else could get in because all the doors were stuck, blocked by fat soldiers and euphoniums and other big instruments. Mrs Owl just flapped about, saying, "Oh dear, oh dear." There was still a smile on her face, but it wasn't a real one.

Someone had to take charge. I thought as people had followed me into the toilet, they'd follow me out again. I ordered what was left of the Royal Marines to get in line. They seemed to think it was all very funny, until I told them to behave. I got all the Brownies and Guides back together and pointing towards the doors at the other end of the supermarket. These other doors opened onto a different road, but that didn't matter, I could still get to the park that way.

"Parade!" I yelled. "One, two, ONE, TWO, THREE, FOUR." We left the supermarket to the sound of only small instruments and tappity drums, but everything was going to be great now, I just knew.

I led the parade onto the other main road *beautifully*, just in time to crash headlong into the Boy Scouts' and Cubs' parade coming the other way!

The road wasn't wide enough for two parades. Our bands and their bands barged into each other like bumper cars at a fairground. Everyone was mixed up. Then our big floats, the ones that hadn't been able to follow us through the supermarket and had gone a different way, bashed into their big floats. Everything came to a stop. The only movement came from my Brownie pack, because we still had sweets to throw – and Cubs to throw them at. And when we ran out of sweets, we threw anything else we could find. And so did they!

★

I didn't think I'd like the Brownies. But now I can't wait to go again. If a walk down the high street could be that much fun, what would camping and *quad biking* be like?

The Ugly Dog
and the Tree

I wish Mum was here more. I know
she has things to do, like building wells
in Africa and saving whales, etc. – but
sometimes I'd like her to be at home.

I was looking at my clothes the other
day. There wasn't anything except old
stuff that was too young for me, or had
holes or was covered in paint – and
nothing fitted, not even nearly. All
my tops and bottoms left my belly
button showing, and they never used
to.

I needed Mum to help choose some new things. After all, I couldn't hang around in my school uniform all day, it's so not-cool. There's a shirt and a skirt and an anorak and shoes, and they're all different sorts of *grey*. When we're in the playground, which is grey too, being concrete, it's like we're in black-and-white and colour hasn't been invented yet.

I needed something dead good – something Jessica Jolly would be really jealous of. Dad wouldn't be any help. He thinks the longer you have the same

28

clothes, the more you like them. He must like his an awful lot, then. Also, he wears an anorak when he doesn't have to!

I couldn't ask Gran to help either. I knew what she'd say. "You have a perfectly good balaclava and mittens that I knitted for you . . . and a scarf and a woolly jumper and leg warmers, and a waistcoat . . . "

I e-mailed Mum. She was somewhere on top of a mountain trying to find the abominable snowman, but she always has her laptop with her and I can write at any time, even when she's in the Himalayas. I told her I needed new clothes. A bit later she e-mailed back.

Annikins,
You caught me in the foothills of Annapurna. The local people here have brought me to a place where they say they often find yeti (abominable snowman)

29

droppings. I'm looking at them now, and I have to believe that's what they are, because these people are yeti-poo experts. I don't know what they do with them – put them on their cabbages perhaps, or light fires with them, but either way I'm not stopping for lunch! I'll be home soon for the Queen's garden party, but I realise you can't wait six whole days. Don't worry though, my lovely, I have passed through some really wonderful countries and bought clothes for you in all of them. I shall send them back by special overnight delivery from the village post office and corner shop! I wish I could be with you when you try everything on.

Kisses
Mum

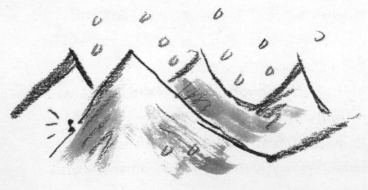

Oh no!
That was *not*
what I wanted.
Last time Mum
sent clothes from
abroad, I didn't
stop scratching for a

week. I think it was the camel-hair top that
gave me the rash, or the horse–hair socks.
Mum never sends *normal* clothes for *normal*
people. The clothes she sends HURT!

The next day was a half-day at school.
Gran was round because it was early closing
and she was out of gargling sherry, she said.
When the man arrived with my parcel, Dad
and Gran watched as I ripped it open. It was
just as bad as I thought it would be. All the
clothes were in different patterns and
colours, and were thick and scratchy. They
didn't bend much either.

Right, I thought, I'll show them. I went
upstairs and put on everything that Mum
had sent, then I added Gran's knitted
balaclava with the peak at the front and

bobble on top, and the gravy-coloured scarf
that trails along the ground behind me. It
was a good thing the weather was cold, or I
would have *fried*.

When I went downstairs again there was
utter silence as they looked at me. Then
there was a long pause, and Dad said,

"I think we'll take a little trip to Wearsons in Sun Street, and see if they have anything a bit more *Annie*. Will you take us, Gran? I could do with a woman's touch."

I wasn't sure Gran had a woman's touch, but I didn't say anything.

While she galloped home to get her motorbike, Grumbler, I went back upstairs to change. I could only find the thin dress I had been wearing before the parcel arrived.

"Where are my clothes, Dad?" I yelled downstairs.

"In the machine," he said. "I thought you'd have plenty of *new* things to wear by now."

We heard Grumbler while Gran was still three streets away, and by the time she arrived I was dressed up again to go out. I looked like a Mongolian yak rider, a Tibetan llama farmer, a mountain-goat herder from wherever mountain goats come from – and someone a bit snake-charmerish, all rolled into one. Then the day got *really* silly.

Dad asked if he could drop off something at the house of a friend of his who lived near Wearsons. It was a big tree in a pot. It had shiny green leaves on, even though it was winter, and it had to stick up through the side-car roof – which didn't leave much room for me.

Halfway to the department store, Grumbler blew up!

Dad shot out of the saddle like a rocket with the legs of his trousers on fire, and Gran had to put him out with a fire extinguisher. He wasn't hurt. Gran also put the engine fire out and gave the bike a good kicking. "You can just stay there until Thursday and the dustman comes!" she told it. "See if I care."

Luckily, we were near a bus stop. Dad wouldn't leave the tree behind in case it was killed by frost, so we hopped on the next bus and took it with us.

Dad's grey trousers were now black and in shreds. I looked like a pile of rugs and Gran looked – well, like Gran. But at least the bus was empty, which was good because otherwise people would have stared. I think the driver was having us on though, because he said, "No trees inside. Trees on top only."

On the front seat upstairs there was a really ugly dog. It was licking the windows and slobbering all over them, so they were

misted up and you couldn't see anything.
But there was nobody with it. We thought it
must belong to the driver, but when we
lugged the tree back downstairs to get off,
the dog followed us and the driver wouldn't
let us leave without it. Then the dog
wouldn't get off the bus so Gran had to
wind the lead round her hand and yank it

along behind her.

When we got to Dad's friend's house, he
was out. All that trouble for nothing. There
was nowhere to leave the tree, so we just
had to keep it. Wearsons was just round the
corner, but it was quite a struggle lugging a
tree and an ugly, grumpy dog up the steps
and through the revolving doors. The
uniformed man inside gave us a frowny look
and Dad said

quickly,
"It's all
right. I'm
not
coming
right in. I'll
just stand
here . . . in
my burnt trousers . . . with my tree . . . and
this bulldog. And you can show my daughter
where the children's clothes are."

"Ah! I get it," said the man, winking at
Dad. "You want the children's fashion show."

"Do I?" asked Dad.

"Yes. Go through that door and along the corridor, and you'll see where to go in."

"But we can't go in looking like this," Dad said.

"Don't worry about that. Anyway, you can't stop here. Bits of your shorts are dropping all over the place. You artistic types, eh?"

Shorts? Poor old Dad. He hadn't realised his trouser legs had completely fallen off and he was wearing what looked like ragged-edged shorts. *And* he had odd socks on. Still, I was glad we'd come. If there was going to be a children's fashion show, with kids wearing the latest gear like you see on TV, Jessica Jolly would be even *more* jealous.

We went through a door and down a gloomy corridor. This wasn't the usual way to the children's department. We followed some arrows to where another man was standing by another door. There was a poster on the wall:

Wearsons Department Store
Kids' & Parents' Fashion Show

"Hurry!" the man called. "You're late. I thought I'd shown everyone in. When a lady and two little girls come out, go through the door – walk along the carpet till you get to the end – and then come back again."

"What's the point of that?" snapped Gran. "We might as well just stay here."

"Ha ha, good joke," said the man. And before we could find out what he meant, the door opened and two kids and a woman came out in *swimming costumes.* Then the man said, "Right! In you go. Don't forget your tree and that ugly dog."

Gran went first, shoving the door open with her bottom, because ugly dog had dug its claws into the carpet and Gran had to pull it through backwards. Dad caught his tree in the door and had to go through backwards too, clutching his pot. The light inside was *blinding* after the dim corridor, and we couldn't see a thing.

So none of us saw all the people.

When my eyes got used to the light, I saw we were on a sort of long, narrow stage with a red carpet on top. We could easily have fallen over the edge due to not seeing where we were going. There were rows of people sitting on both sides, but we were the only ones lit up. It almost looked as if they were clapping and cheering *us*. We've come in the wrong door, I thought. This was where the people modelling the clothes walked up and down.

Of course, Gran realised what was happening very quickly when she turned round. This was an audience – and you know what she's like with an audience. She took up her "Greek statue" pose. It was difficult, because although she was standing still pretending she was playing an invisible harp, the dog started pulling her sideways, rucking up the carpet like a

ploughed field. Anyway, the statue effect was
spoilt because Greek goddesses don't wear
thick leather coats, leather helmets, goggles
and boots.

The audience loved it though.

Dad was trying to make himself invisible
behind the tree. Gran gave him the dog's
lead so she could strut up and down better
– opening her coat to let everyone see her
tracksuit top with the sleeveless cardigan

41

over it – but Dad couldn't hold the pot and the dog. He dumped the tree on the carpet and the dog peed on it. I wish I hadn't followed them through the door. I could've been halfway home by then.

I put my sulky look on. It was weird, but after a few steps, I couldn't help doing that strange walk models use, crossing one leg in front of the other. But I had big boots on, from Kurdistan, I think, so I was *clumping*, not walking, and I kept tripping over my own feet. But I got the biggest cheer of all, and I could hear people saying, "They've left the best till last!" and "What a wonderful combination of textures." Whatever that means.

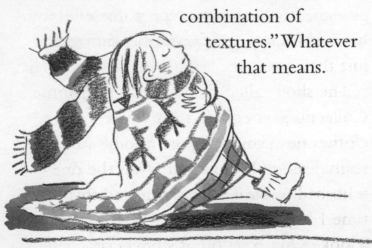

When Gran and I got to the end of the runway, we turned and met Dad again on the way back. Gran took the dog's lead, and Dad picked up the tree, and I tripped over one last time and got another cheer. Then we were outside again in the corridor.

Newspaper cameramen took pictures of me in front of the store with the ugly dog and the tree. It was on the fashion page the week after.

Later, Mum brought over a big lorry-load of clothes for Wearsons to sell. She likes doing things like that so that poor people who make the clothes can earn money and buy colour televisions. And it made up for her not finding an abominable snowman – just their poo!

The shop called the clothes "The Annie Collection". I couldn't NOT wear the clothes now, could I? Jessica Jolly was really jealous, I know, but I was the one who had to wear everything, and this time I had rashes in *three* different colours. I looked like a scoop of strawberry-

and–chocolate–ripple ice–cream. But it was worth it.

The paper said I was the coolest kid in town!

Robo–Mop

Every year, our school asks us to do a project with our families. They usually copy the ideas from a TV programme. This year, they wanted us to make a robot. It sounded fun, but no way could *my* family make one.

Miss Felton said, "Not all families will want to take part, but we can all share in the excitement when the families battle it out for 'Best Robot' prize."

"It won't be our family that wins it," I said to Gran. "There's only you who knows about making things, and you're old, and Mum isn't around, and Dad's useless with machines."

Gran glared at me. "Old, am I? You don't know much, Annie Fidgen . . . and you don't know much about your father! You don't even know what his job is."

"He hasn't got a job," I replied. "He grows carrots and plays with his computer. The end."

Gran doesn't get angry very often – but she was now.

"Fat lot you know then, young lady!" she shouted. "Listen to me . . . 'playing with computers' *is* his job. Your dad is very clever. He might not be able to put up a deckchair, or use a Hoover, but he knows everything there is to know about computers."

"Dad? – *My* dad?"

"Yes, your dad. He invents things. If anyone can design a robot, he can. And, as old as I am, I can build it." She puffed herself up. "I can take a double-decker bus to bits with a sack over my head."

"You can't!"

"I learned in the army."

Gran surprises me sometimes with all the things she's done. "You were in the army?" I asked.

"Before I became an actress, yes."

"You were an *actress*?"

"See! You don't know anything about anything."

I rang Jessica Jolly. "Did you get an instruction sheet about the robots?"

"Sure," she said, "didn't you?"

"No. I thought my
family would be
useless, so I
didn't take one.
What did it
say?"

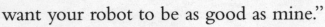

"Why should
I tell you?" she
said, nastily. "I don't
want your robot to be as good as mine."

"Don't tell me then!"

"Anyway, there weren't many rules. Your
robot can do anything – "

"What does that mean?" I interrupted.
"That it can use *any* kind of weapon?"

"Weapon?"

"Yes, you know, what weapons can we give the robots? Chainsaws, flame-throwers, what?"

There was a long pause. "Oh yes, flame-throwers," she said, "like in *Robot Wars*! Well, it didn't say you *couldn't* use flame-throwers. Or axes . . . or a machine-gun . . . You could use a machine-gun."

"You're just being stupid," I said.

Dad asked me what sort of robot I wanted him to design, and I told him. I wanted something really evil-looking with a spike at the front to stab the enemy robots and tip them upside down, a huge hammer to smash them to bits, and a circular saw to slice them up, and . . .

"Whoa, hold on," Dad said. "This is not a friendly robot, is it? Are you sure I shouldn't be designing something that sharpens pencils for you or plays hopscotch?"

"I want a CRUNCHER, Dad, like you see on TV."

★

We used bits of junk from Gran's garage to make the robot. When Dad had finished on the computer, I took the plans to Gran. She put on a huge welding helmet and heavy motorcycling gloves. Then there were lots of sparks, and Gran was lit up from underneath like she was in a horror film. She welded bits of washing machine to bits of caravan

and added a bike chain to something off
a fridge – and wheels. She put on the
battle hammer and the spikes, and some
snapping teeth, and a long arm with
two elbows.

It looked a bit like a crab, and a bit like a
rhinoceros on wheels. Then she tried
everything out by touching different wires

to the battery. The robot spun around and snapped its mouth.

"That'll do," she said.

Then it was Dad's turn again and he put in 'the brains'. When everything was finished, we tried it out in Gran's garden. It was *awesome*! Mr Kravitz's fence was turned into matchsticks – and there wasn't a flowerpot or a garden gnome left in one piece!

I hadn't done anything yet! But now I sprayed on red and yellow flames with car paint, and painted the pointed teeth – and four red, staring eyes.

Scare-eee! I couldn't wait for the big battle.

When the day came, we went to school on Grumbler, Gran's motorbike. I had to sit next to the robot on top of tools and stuff.

Loudspeakers crackled, and a voice said, "FIFTEEN MINUTES!"

Billy Williams's family was near. His dad is a cook. Dad called me over to them and pointed down. On the ground was a shoebox on wheels, and it had an arm waving around with a fork on the end of it and a sausage! I laughed. That wouldn't last ten seconds in the ring! Dad went over to the next team and pointed again. They had a robot that bumbled about, and when it hit someone's legs it turned, and went in another direction.

"Dad," I said. "These are pathetic. We'll slaughter them!"

Dad didn't say anything. He just pointed to a huge banner covering half the school:

Glendale Primary School
Domestic Robot Competition

"What?"

"*Domestic* robot, Annie."

"Yes," I agreed. "The Glendale Primary School Domestic Robot Competition." Then I thought about it. "What does 'domestic' mean?"

Gran said, "Stupid girl! It means jobs around the house, like cleaning and tidying. We can't put our robot in the ring now. It'll *exterminate* them!"

"TEN MINUTES!" said the loudspeakers.

"You have to fix it then, Gran." I wailed. "Change it into a domestic cleaning up and tidying robot – please, Gran! You've got to . . . "

Dad said, "There's no time, Annie. They'll be starting soon . . . What do you think, Gran?"

Gran said doubtfully, "I could get rid of the spike and hammer and make it look a bit less fierce."

"And I could program it to do cleaning movements. All right, let's see what we can do, but really I need more time."

I went to ask the woman with the clock for a few more minutes, but when I went in her little tent, she was looking the other way, so I just moved the hands of the clock back a bit and waltzed out again, whistling.

Ten minutes later, the speaker said,
"TWELVE MINUTES?" in a puzzled
voice.

Then, who do you think I saw?

"MUM!" I yelled, and ran towards her.
Mum turned and smiled. She was in a
crowd of people wanting her autograph, as
usual, because she's — you know, famous. But
she rushed over and gave me a big hug.

"I thought I'd surprise you, Annikins," she
said. "I'm sorry I always miss your special
days, but I'm here now, and dying to see
your robot."

"Yes, well . . . "

"Where're Dad and Gran?"

The crowd was still trying to get Mum's

attention, but over their heads you could see Gran's welder like a giant sparkler, and hear

some really loud grinding, banging and drilling noises.

"Over there," I nodded.

"FIVE MINUTES!"

"I'd better take my seat," Mum said. "I'll see you later." The whole crowd moved off with her. I'd almost forgotten Mum was the famous adventurer. I mean . . . she's just Bizzy Lizzie, *my mum*.

A bit of the playground had a little wall around it. That's where everyone was going. Miss Felton ticked off names in a notebook as the teams put their robots in the ring. Jessica Jolly put in a really droopy-looking robot. It was pink, with clothes painted on and sunglasses. One arm had a feather duster and another had a mop. She grinned at me and pointed to the word "Domestic" on the wall. She'd known what it meant – she'd read the instructions.

"Did you find a machine-gun?" she asked sweetly.

"And what is your robot called, Jessica?" asked the teacher.

"Mrs Mop, Miss Felton."

Huh! Pathetic name too! Miss Felton wrote it down, and just as the last team put their robot into the ring and went away,

Dad and Gran rushed up as if they'd run a hundred miles.

"Can we . . . phew . . . borrow a dustbin?" Dad asked, out of puff.

"I suppose so . . . Why has your robot got sharp teeth and red eyes, Mr Fidgen?" Miss Felton asked.

"It's to frighten the dirt!" Gran said quickly. "Our machine is very hard on dirt."

"It is a *domestic* robot, isn't it? I mean, it looks like one of those Battle Robots on television."

"Course it's domestic!" snapped Gran. "It's got a broom."

It had as well – a big playground broom where the sledgehammer had been – and a shovel. It was four times the size of any other robot, but Gran had tied a pinny around it to make it look pretty.

It didn't though. It looked *angry*.

Gran went off to find the dustbin.

"It just cleans up things," I told Miss Felton. "It's very *domestic*."

"Does it have a name, Annie?"

"Yes, it's called . . . " Oh, no . . . I couldn't tell her it was called CRUSHER! I thought of Jessica Jolly's Mrs Mop. "ROBO-MOP!" I said.

"OK then," Miss Felton said. "Put it in the ring with the others."

Most of the others looked like *toy* robots like you buy in shops, with extra bits stuck

on. One was a little blue fluffy bunny that banged two tins together! Nobody had *invented* anything, or gone to any trouble. Not like we had.

Miss Felton blew a whistle. I switched on Robo-Mop and jumped out. Dad looked worried. Our robot started racing around like a mad thing, banging its broom and shovel together and *roaring* like a lion.

"Sorry," Dad whispered. "I didn't have time to change everything. It still thinks it's the Terminator."

Some of the robots were hardly moving. Tomas Flem's robot, Jenny the Housemaid, was turning slowly in circles, waving a feather duster in the air. Roy Pawson's radio-controlled truck had a scrubbing-brush taped underneath it, and he was using a remote control to make it go backwards and forwards.

But nobody was looking at them. They were all looking at Robo-Mop.

It had stopped racing around now and had backed up against the wall, but it was still bashing its broom and shovel together and bouncing around on its springs like it couldn't wait to start *cleaning up*!

Suddenly it leaped forward, turning around like it was wondering where to start. Mrs Mop made a big mistake and tried to *dust* it. Robo-Mop whacked Mrs Mop so

hard with the broom, it made a dent in the playground. The broom must have still thought it was a hammer.

"Hey, that's not fair," Jessica Jolly yelled. I smiled – but only on the inside. Well, there was nothing I could do. It wasn't my fault – I only painted it.

Robo-Mop went completely crazy then, bashing robots left and right with its broom like it was swatting flies, and flipping them upside-down. Then, one at a time, it scooped them up on the shovel, lifted the lid of the dustbin, and tipped them in. And when the last one had gone into the bin, Robo-Mop slammed the lid back on, calmly moved to the centre of the ring and switched itself off. Nobody made a sound. They were all too dazed to move, staring at Robo-Mop with their mouths open.

"There!" I said to myself. "It does clean up."

Miss Felton didn't want to give me the prize, I could tell, but I *always* win, don't I? And who else could she give it to? My robot was the only one left.

Gran was pleased with herself, dancing around and punching the air, but Dad went

to all the other families offering to mend their robots. I think most of them had enjoyed themselves really, except Mrs Jolly, Jessica's mum, who found she was allergic to robots.

And Jessica Jolly didn't speak to me for a week.

Good!

A Friend for Life

Last weekend I was round at Gran's. She was taking a television to bits. There was wire and stuff all over the tablecloth. I'd gone to ask if she knew someone who would take Ugly for a walk. Gran was being difficult.

"Mrs Gillespie," I suggested.

"No!" said Gran.

"One of your friends at The Horse and Cart, then."

"Not them either." she said. "They don't walk dogs. You'll have to do it yourself."

"Why do I have to?" I asked. "It's not my dog. You and Dad found her at the same time as me. Why can't you take her?"

"Because."

"Because what?"

"Because I've got a bone in my leg."

Gran always says that when she doesn't want to do something. "You don't have a bone in your leg when you're down at the pub disco night!" I accused her.

"That's different," she said. "These are dancing legs, not walking legs . . . "

There was no way I was going to win an argument with Granny Weatherburn. Especially when it was about the dog. I couldn't find out where Ugly had come from and I couldn't give her away. No one wanted a fat, lazy bulldog. But I'm a caring

66

person. I wanted somebody old to take the dog out because old people don't do anything any more and have weak legs. It would do them good to walk a dog and think about someone else for a change.

I tried again.

"Mr Kravitz?"

"No," said Gran.

I have tried to take Ugly out myself, honestly, but she doesn't like moving about. She doesn't run after balls. She doesn't chase cats or fetch sticks. She just looks at me like I'm mad when I throw a rubber bone and yell "Fetch!" and then run off to pick it up myself, and throw it again ...

I don't need a dog. She's not mine. She's a waste of space.

"Mr Alexander?" I asked.

"No."

Usually I like animals better than people. People like Roy Pawson, for instance – who I especially don't like, because he thinks he's funny when he's not. But this dog is worse than Roy Pawson. She stinks. She scratches all the time she's not asleep, and evil smells come from her bottom. She eats anything you put on the floor: cabbage, curried spinach, taramasalata, as well as real food and anything that is already on the floor, like shoes. She even eats radishes! What sort of dog eats radishes? But you have to put the food in front of her. She won't get up for it. She eats lying down and then falls asleep with her head in the bowl.

"Gran, what are you doing to the TV?"

She looked up. "I'm trying to find out if there's anything in there besides gardening and cookery programmes."

That was *stupid*! "Is that a joke?" I asked.

Gran said, "*Tsss!* You wouldn't know a joke if it bit your bum. Yes, it was a joke. I'm fixing it for Mr Kravitz so he can get Polish television by satellite."

"You can do that?" I asked, amazed.

"I don't see why not. I've never tried before. You don't know what you can do till you try. My cousin Norman could fix televisions, and he was bonkers. He used to stand on one leg on Thursdays, and he sometimes played an organ in the middle of the road. If *he* could mend televisions, how hard can it be?"

"But what are these bits you've taken out?" I asked, pointing to all the stuff.

"Well, the things in this pile I call 'yellow bits', and those in that pile are called 'blue bits'. Those green wiggly things are called 'green wiggly things'. The other bits I don't know."

As I left, Gran said, "Why don't you take the dog to the Sunnydale Dogs' Home. They'll find a good home for her." That sounded like a good idea.

I'd invented a way to take Ugly out to do her business, but it needed patience and a

wheelbarrow. I need a wheelbarrow for lots of things. But I couldn't lug a barrowful of bulldog all the way to the dogs' home on my own, so Dad came with me. The place

was in the high street: a big red house with
lots of fat trees in the front. An important-
looking man opened the door. I asked him
where all the dogs were.

"We have kennels at the back, young
lady," he said. He sounded like he didn't like
talking to a *girl*. He turned to Dad. "Did you
wish to look for a dog?" he asked. The man
hadn't noticed the barrow then.

"No, we want to give you one," Dad said.

"Very well," sniffed the man. "We find
excellent homes for *every* dog that comes
here." He was very snooty.

Dad was looking at the potted plants by

the door, so I pushed the barrow into the hall. The man looked down at it in horror.

"Ugh . . . That dog *again*! When I said we find homes for *every* dog," he said, holding his nose, "I meant every dog *except that one*!"

"But she's very cute," I told him, crossing my fingers behind my back. "She's no trouble."

"She *is* trouble, little girl."

I hate being called *little girl*!

"We've had that dog here four times!" he went on. "That's our collar and lead she's wearing. We don't ever want her back. The reasons are: one – she knows how to open the fridge door and eats everything she can reach."

He was counting off the reasons on his fingers – I hate people who do that.

"Two – she won't let the vet see her. Three – she jams her back against the wall so we can't pick her up to scrub her clean. Four – the other dogs catch her fleas and diseases. And five – she chews through the wire netting and lets herself and all the other dogs out. Then, when all hell has been let loose, she calmly waits at the stop outside for a 39 bus! No – I'm sorry, she can't stay here. I have my other dogs to think about."

I looked at the other dogs before we left. They were all squeaky clean and on their best behaviour, and they wagged their tails when they saw me. Cute. Then I went back to the ugly lump lying in the wheelbarrow, wheezing and snorting and blowing nose-bubbles. She raised her head from her paws long enough to sneeze all over the important man, and then went back to sleep, drooling into the barrow.

And suddenly I quite liked her.

The man couldn't get rid of us fast enough. He gave us some dog stuff to take away. Stuff for fleas and for lots of things I hadn't heard of, like ticks and ear-mites, canker and mange and tapeworms and roundworms and everything else a dog can

catch. My dog had the lot. Did I say "my dog"? I didn't mean it. She's not mine – just an ugly old fleabag we found on a bus.

When we got home, I scrubbed her with

some flea-killing soap while she was still in the barrow. She looked up at me sadly and groaned, as if to say, "You must be joking!" I sprayed her with some other gunk and puffed some powder over her, and when she was done, I dumped her out on the lawn. I gave her the tablets. She just ate them like they were Smarties. She didn't look any better, but she wasn't quite so pongy.

Dad complained that she kept lying on his carrots, and said I'd have to take her to obedience classes. It's like dogs have their own school! Jessica Jolly said there's an animal trainer in Enfield who used to be on television. She takes her rabbit Robbie there when he gets out of control. She said this woman can train *anything* in five minutes!

I'd like to see her try with Ugly.

Jessica Jolly helped me lug the dog-barrow over to Turkey Street, where the training hall is. There were some other people outside when we got there. Their dogs were pulling them in all directions and snarling and fighting each other. One dog didn't have any lips — just teeth! They didn't mess with Ugly though. When the doors opened, we all dragged our dogs inside, across the slippery floor. Some dogs went the long way round, going out one door and coming back through another, towing people behind them like they were skaters on the shiny lino. It was crazy. At least Ugly didn't do that. All she did was snort.

The trainer's name was Willie Meena Googlies, or that's what it sounded like. She had a funny accent and talked in little bitty sentences. She had hairy legs and wore men's shoes.

Everyone had to write their name and their dog's name on a badge and pin it to their clothes. Mrs Googlies made us stand in a line with the dogs and then she said, "SIT!" very loudly. Four people sat on the floor before we realised she meant the dogs.

"Very good, Annie," she said. Ugly was the only dog sitting. But she'd already been sitting! It's her second-favourite position after lying down. Then we had to yell

"STAY!"
and walk
away from
our dogs.
"Very good,
Annie!" she said
again. All the other
dogs had followed
their owners, but
Ugly was still where
I'd left her. Getting
her to stay had never
been a problem.
Getting her to go
was the hard thing.
We were there for

an hour. We didn't have any lessons in *going*. Just *sitting* and *staying*. What good was that? That was all Ugly ever did!

After the lesson, Mrs Googlies said Ugly was "well-behaving". Fat lot she knows. "Doggy is bored!" she said. "You need to make for her interest! Play with. Also she will not like name you give. Dogs is people too, you know."

Jessica Jolly wasn't much use. All she did was giggle.

Ugly didn't have a name. Only what I called her. And how can dogs get bored? They get excited at the same things dumb boys do, don't they? Trees, and dirt, and balls. Ugly is just interested in different things that's all – like sleeping. And radishes.

When we got home at last, Ugly wouldn't come in. Instead she wandered round the garden, poking about in the shed and scratching the ground. I'd never seen her move because she wanted to before.

I sighed. I didn't want a dog. But I had a dog.

Wrong!

Next morning I didn't have a dog. I had SIX!

In the night, Ugly had crawled under Dad's workbench, where there are lots of wood shavings and rags and paint tins and stuff – *and had five puppies!* No wonder she had been eating radishes – that's what Mum said she'd wanted to eat when she was expecting me! Ugly looked really pleased with herself. The puppies looked just like her – except they weren't ugly at all! They were gorgeous!

I shot round to Gran's to tell her the news, but she was next door. I could see her through the window. She was standing on a chair waving a satellite dish. It looked like she'd got Mr Kravitz's TV working, but the picture was upside down and Mr Kravitz was standing on his head on the sofa, looking at it.

They looked busy, but I just had to tell somebody . . .

That my dog – *my* dog – my very

own clever, ugly dog, had five beautiful
puppies!

(P.S. She's not that ugly, actually.)